THE DRAGON RIDERS

A Dragon Brothers Book

James Russell
Link Choi

sourcebooks
jabberwocky

Away across the oceans,
where few have dared to roam,
upon a wondrous island,
a family made its home.

Young brothers, Flynn and Paddy,
as you can plainly see
are lovers of adventure
and happy as can be.

The boys had not a notion
(until quite recently)
that dragons roamed across their land
in startling quantities.

SEE THE MAP IN THIS BOOK
COME ALIVE!

1. Download the free **AR Reads** app on your Android- or iOS- compatible smartphone or tablet.

2. Launch the app and hover your device over the map to explore Flynn and Paddy's interactive world. See and hear dragons fly, fire crackle, and get a glimpse of your favorite characters in action!

But on their last excursion,
they'd got one for a pet.
The trouble was they didn't know
quite what to feed him yet.

He often stole poor Coco's bone
and munched it in a flash.
But Paddy's spinach sandwiches
were promptly turned to ash.

The dragon, whom they'd given
the name of Elton John,
was kept in several secret spots
until their mom had gone.

That became much harder when
the dragon grew, of course.
He'd grown so tall he'd easily
look down upon a horse.

One day, when they were playing
(while keeping out of sight),
Elton grabbed the three of them
and took off into flight.

Paddy laughed, Flynn grew mad,
and Coco yelped and whined,
but Elton kept on flying
and paid them little mind.

They flew across the Putrid Plains
and saw the Boiling Stream.
Since Elton loved to warm himself,
he flew right through the steam.

They passed the Magic Terraces—
gleaming white and pink—
and when they skimmed above a lake,
their dragon took a drink.

Clever Elton somehow knew
the path he had to follow.
A natural instinct told him—
like a warbler or a swallow.

A monstrous flock of dragons
were gathered for the games,
which every year are planned with care
but always end in flames.

According to tradition,
only dragons were allowed.
So, naturally, young boys and dogs
stood right out from the crowd.

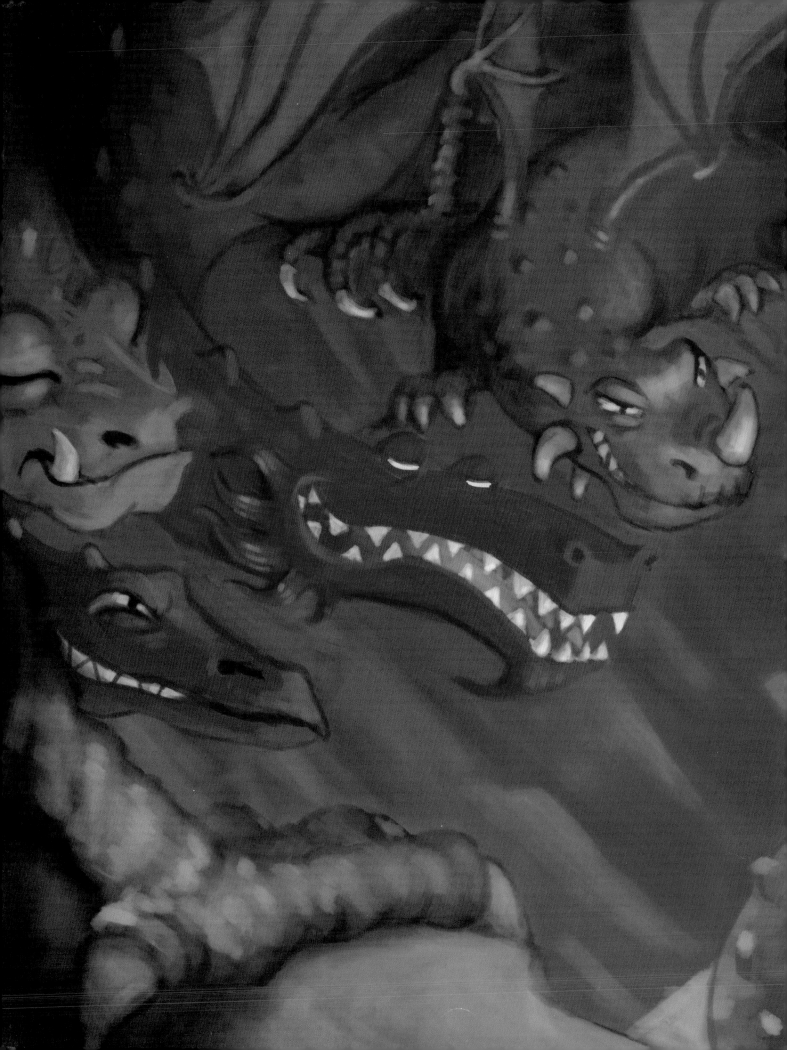

The dragons gnashed their fearsome teeth,
and then the chase was on.
But never had they tried to catch
the likes of Elton John.

He spread his wings and dived so fast
the boys could scarcely see.
Poor Coco, hanging down below,
just barely missed a tree.

Their dragon changed direction
and flew into the sky.
The boys could only just hold on
as startled birds flew by.

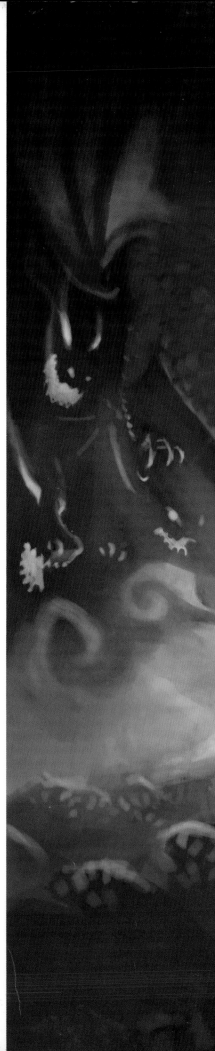

Heavenward they hurtled
at a terrifying speed.
They'd never gone this fast before
(the brothers both agreed).

Elton saw his only chance,
and with a dragon's grin,
he plunged inside the Constant Cloud.
"Good thinking!" cried out Flynn.

Enveloped by the swirling mist,
they couldn't see a thing.
But all around, the strangest sounds
went CRASH and BANG and PING!

The chasing pack of dragons,
unsure of where to fly,
all crashed into each other
and fell out of the sky!

Emerging from the Constant Cloud,
the boys let forth a cheer.
"Hooray for Elton John," they whooped,
"the fastest dragon here!"

The boys were so excited.
They longed to tell their mom
about how brave and clever
their dragon had become.

At home their mother smiled a smile
and spoke, "It's time for bed.
Good night, you dragon brothers,"
she sweetly, softly said.

Just before they fell asleep,
they heard a distant roaring.
But warm as toast inside their beds,
in seconds they were snoring.

THE END

Adobe Photoshop was used to prepare the full color art.

Published by Sourcebooks Jabberwocky, an imprint of Sourcebooks, Inc.
P.O. Box 4410, Naperville, Illinois 60567-4410
(630) 961-3900
Fax: (630) 961-2168
www.sourcebooks.com

Originally published in 2014 in New Zealand by Dragon Brothers Ltd.

Library of Congress Cataloging-in-Publication data is on file with the publisher.

Source of Production: Leo Paper, Heshan City, Guangdong Province, China
Date of Production: April 2017
Run Number: 5009161

Printed and bound in China.
LEO 10 9 8 7 6 5 4 3 2 1

For my mum

—JR

For Dallas, as always

—LC

The Dragon Riders is the third book in
The Dragon Brothers series. To find out more about
Flynn and Paddy's world visit www.dragonbrothersbooks.com.

THE ADVENTURE CONTINUES!

Be on the lookout
for books 1 and 2 in the
Dragon Brothers series!

THE DRAGON HUNTERS

Living on an island means life is full of adventure for brothers Flynn and Paddy. So when a dragon swoops out of the sky and nabs Coco, their beloved dog, Flynn and Paddy know it's up to them to bring her home. That night, they pack their bags, make some terrible sandwiches, and set off on an epic adventure...

THE DRAGON TAMERS

When Flynn and Paddy discover a strange map that shows magical-sounding landmarks all around their island home, they decide it's time to go exploring! But when they unexpectedly stumble across a dragon hatchery, the brothers end up going home with more than a good story...

EXPERiENCE THE MAGIC—iN 3D!

You've read the story; now watch it unfold before your eyes! Join the dragons and soar above Flynn and Paddy's magical island home as your imagination comes to life! Cutting-edge augmented reality technology brings their world off the page and into yours. All it takes is **two simple steps:**

1. Download the free AR Reads app on your Android- or iOS-compatible smartphone or tablet.

2. Launch the app and hover your device over the map to explore Flynn and Paddy's interactive world. See and hear dragons fly, fire crackle, and get a glimpse of your favorite characters in action!

Don't have a smartphone or tablet? Visit **dragonbrothersbooks.com** to watch a video on how the augmented reality works.

About the Author and Illustrator

James Russell, an author and journalist from New Zealand, was blessed to spend his childhood holidaying in the wilderness—from the coast, to the pristine inland lakes, to the towering mountain ranges of the South Island.

It's those majestic and mystical places, their flora and fauna, and the sense of adventure he felt in exploring them that form the backdrop of much of his writing today.

Inspiration also comes from observing the humor, imagination, and carefree spirit of his own two young boys as they discover the natural world around them. He is married to Rebecca and lives in Auckland.

Link Choi was a finalist for the Russell Clark Medal for Illustration for his work on *The Dragon Hunters*. When he is not reading or making picture books, he helps create the look of films such as the Hobbit trilogy. He lives in Auckland, New Zealand.

DRAGON HATCHERY

DRAGON'S LAIR

MT. MONSTROUS

RIDGE OF RISING FLAME

SWAMP OF CHILDREN'S WISHES

TREE OF WAILING WITCHES

RICKETY TRAIL

MEADOW OF DREAMS

ANCIENT FOREST

FLYNN & PADDY'S HOUSE

MYSTIC MO

N
W   E
S